¿QUE VOLA, NOLA?
WHAT'S UP, NOLA?

Abigail Isaacoff

Illustrated by
Ramiro Díaz

PELICAN PUBLISHING
NEW ORLEANS 2021

Library of Congress Cataloging-in-Publication Data

Names: Isaacoff, Abigail, author. | Díaz, Ramiro, 1983- illustrator.
Title: Que vola, NOLA? What's up, NOLA? / Abigail Isaacoff ; illustrated by
  Ramiro Díaz.
Description: New Orleans : Pelican Publishing, 2021. | Summary: "A lizard from
  Havana winds up in New Orleans and since it is so similar, he thinks he is just
  in a different part of Havana. Bilingual text, English and Spanish"— Provided
  by publisher.
Identifiers: LCCN 2020008745 | ISBN 9781455625383 (hardback) | ISBN
  9781455625390 (ebook)
Subjects: CYAC: Lizards—Fiction. | Havana (Cuba)—Fiction. | Cuba—Fiction.
  | New Orleans (La.)—Fiction. | Spanish language materials—Bilingual.
Classification: LCC PZ73 .I726 2021 | DDC [E]—dc23
LC record available at https://lccn.loc.gov/2020008745

Printed in Korea
Published by Pelican Publishing
New Orleans, LA
www.pelicanpub.com

To Eli, Wolfgang, Zebulon, Opal, and all of the children of the United States, Latin America, and the world. Special thanks to dear sister Jessica!

Ramito was an anole, a little lizard. He lived in the city of Havana, on the island of Cuba. *¿Que vola, Ramito?* What's up, Ramito?

Ramito fue un anole, un lagarto pequeño. El vivió en la ciudad de la Habana, en la isla de Cuba. ¿Que vola, Ramito?

Ramito was a happy lizard in Havana. Every morning, he would wake up in his Ceiba tree and sunbathe. When he was warm enough, he would have a breakfast of *cafecito* (Cuban coffee) and big gross bugs. They are gross to you but not to Ramito! Then, he would explore the city.

Ramito fue un lagarto feliz en la Habana. Cada mañana, él se despertaba en su Ceiba y tomaba el sol. Cuando el estaba suficientemente cálido, el tendría un desayuno de café y bichos grandes y asquerosos. ¡Son asquerosos para ti, pero no para Ramito! Luego, exploraba la ciudad.

Ramito loved Havana. He loved the old buildings and the busy streets.

Ramito amaba la Habana. Amaba los edificios viejos y las calles concurridas.

On a beautiful day, he loved to go to the *Malecón* (Wall) by the sea with his friends.

En un lindo día, le encantaba ir al Malecón con sus amigos.

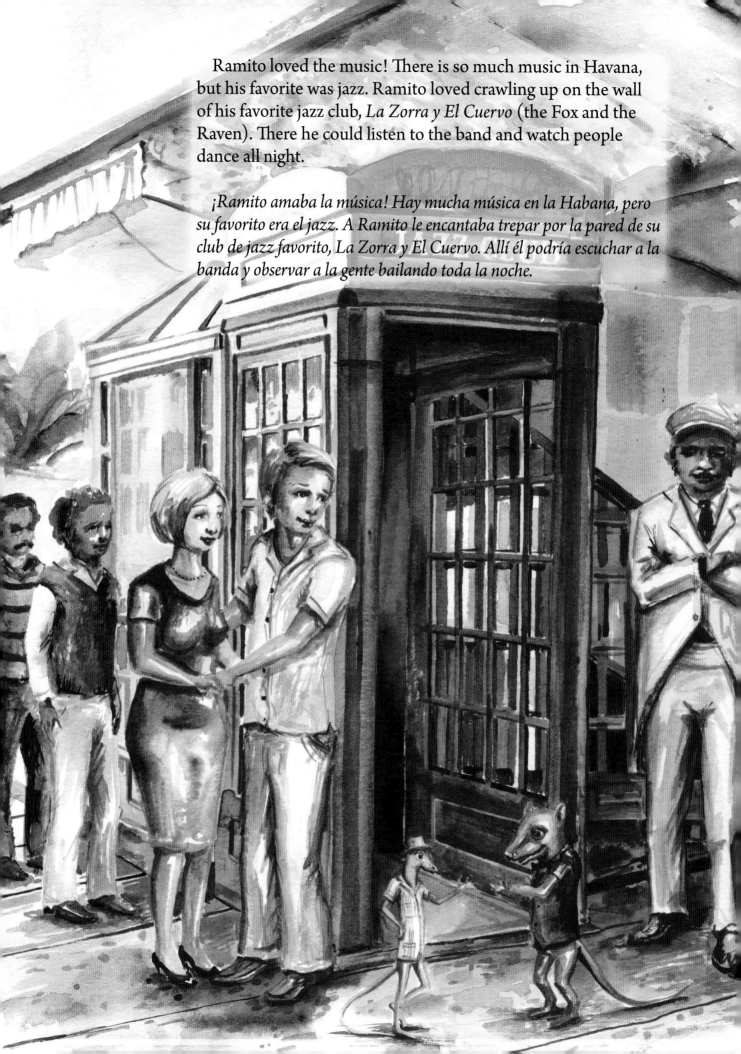

Ramito loved the music! There is so much music in Havana, but his favorite was jazz. Ramito loved crawling up on the wall of his favorite jazz club, *La Zorra y El Cuervo* (the Fox and the Raven). There he could listen to the band and watch people dance all night.

¡Ramito amaba la música! Hay mucha música en la Habana, pero su favorito era el jazz. A Ramito le encantaba trepar por la pared de su club de jazz favorito, La Zorra y El Cuervo. Allí él podría escuchar a la banda y observar a la gente bailando toda la noche.

Ramito started noticing more and more visitors to his city. People came from all over the world to experience the beauty of his island. One afternoon, Ramito heard jazz music coming from an open window at a hotel. He climbed inside the window to hear it better. The music was coming from a record player. The music was soft and sweet. It made Ramito happy but sleepy.

Ramito comenzó a notar más y más visitantes a su ciudad. Personas llegaban de todas partes del mundo para ver la belleza de su isla. Una tarde, Ramito escuchó música de jazz desde una ventana abierta de un hotel. Él se trepó adentro para escucharla mejor. La música venía de un tocadiscos. La música era suave y dulce. Lo hizo feliz pero soñoliento.

Ramito found a place to take a nap.

Ramito encontró un lugar para tomarse una siesta.

It was a very long nap.

Fue una siesta muy larga.

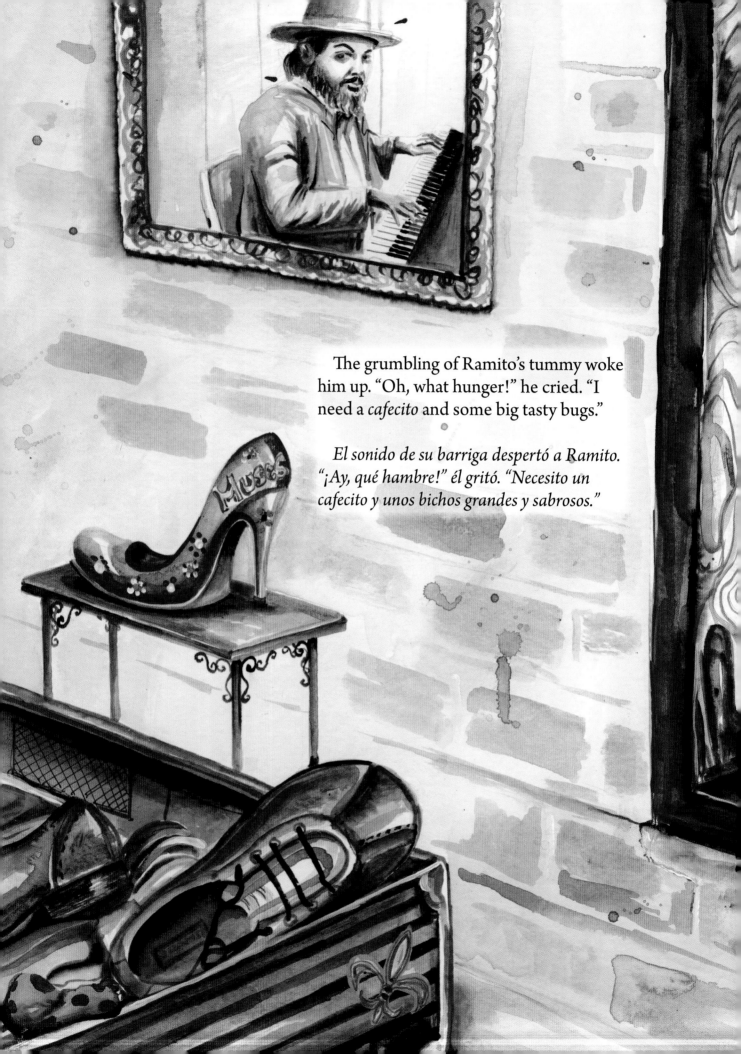

The grumbling of Ramito's tummy woke him up. "Oh, what hunger!" he cried. "I need a *cafecito* and some big tasty bugs."

El sonido de su barriga despertó a Ramito. "¡Ay, qué hambre!" él gritó. "Necesito un cafecito y unos bichos grandes y sabrosos."

Ramito went to the open window and looked around. "Why, this is not my neighborhood," he said. "It looks familiar, though. I know! I will find a friend and ask for directions back o my Ceiba tree."

Ramito fue a la ventana abierta y miró a su alrededor. "Pues, te no es mi barrio," él dijo. "Me parece muy familiar. ¡Yo se! Voy a contrar a un amigo y pedirle direcciones de vuelta a mi Ceiba."

Ramito climbed out the window and down the wall to the street. There, in a spot of sunshine, he met another lizard. "*Hola. ¿Que vola, asere?* Hello. What's up, buddy? My name is Ramito, and I seem to be lost. I do not know this street. Can you help me find my Ceiba tree? And perhaps a *cafecito* and some big tasty bugs? I'm hungry and I want to eat."

"Hello, Ramito, my name is Bernard," said the other lizard. "It sounds like you are very lost. But we always depend on the kindness of strangers in this city. So I will try my very best to help you. Here, you can share these palmetto bugs with me."

"*Cucarachas!* My favorite!" cried Ramito.

Ramito salió por la ventana y bajó la pared a la calle. Allí, en un lugar soleado, conoció a otro lagarto. "Hola. ¿Que vola, asere? Me llamo Ramito, y creo que estoy perdido. Yo no conozco esta calle. ¿Puedes ayudarme encontrar mi Ceiba? ¿Y quizás un cafecito y unos bichos grandes y sabrosos? Yo tengo hambre y quiero jamar."

"Hola, Ramito, me llamo Bernard," dijo el otro lagarto. "Parece que estás muy perdido. Pero siempre dependemos de la caridad de extraños en esta ciudad. Así que haré todo lo posible para ayudarte. Mira, puedes compartir estos insectos conmigo."

"¡Cucarachas! Mis favoritas!" gritó Ramito.

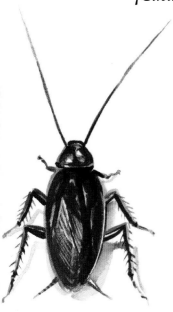

"And now let me take you to my favorite place for coffee."

Ramito and Bernard sipped a *café au lait* and listened to a saxophone.

"I love the saxophone!" said Ramito. "I can hear one like this from my Ceiba tree. Where are we in Old Havana?"

"So sorry, my friend," said Bernard. "I have never heard of Havana. We are in New Orleans, Louisiana—NOLA."

"No way!" cried Ramito. "This is clearly Havana, Cuba. Why, I think I hear the bell of the *Catedral de San Cristóbal.*"

"We are near a cathedral. I can take you there," said Bernard.

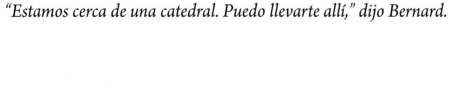

"Y ahora déjame llevarte a mi lugar favorito para tomar café."

Ramito y Bernard sorbieron un cafe au lait *y escucharon al saxofón.*

"¡Me encanta el saxofón!" dijo Ramito. "Puedo oír uno como este de mi Ceiba. ¿Dónde estamos en la Habana Vieja?"

"Lo siento, mi amigo," dijo Bernard. "Yo nunca escuché de la Habana. Estamos en Nueva Orleans, Louisiana—NOLA."

"¡No es posible!" gritó Ramito. "Esto es claramente la Habana, Cuba. Creo que puedo oír la campana de La Catedral de San Cristóbal."

"Estamos cerca de una catedral. Puedo llevarte allí," dijo Bernard.

"Why, this is a plaza, but not the *Plaza de la Catedral*," said Ramito, scratching his head. "It looks familiar, Bernard. But I have never seen this church before."

"Ramito, this is St. Louis Cathedral. We are in Jackson Square," said Bernard.

"Square! That is a silly word," said Ramito with a laugh. "I have never been in this part of Old Havana."

"Pues, esta es una plaza, pero no la Plaza de la Catedral," dijo Ramito, rascándose la cabeza. *"Parece familiar, Bernard. Pero yo nunca he visto esta iglesia antes."*

"Ramito, esta es la Catedral de San Luis. Estamos en Jackson Square," dijo Bernard.

"¡Square! ¡Qué palabra más tonta!" se río Ramito. *"Yo nunca he estado en esta parte de la Habana Vieja."*

"Ramito!" cried Bernard. "You are confused. You are not in Old Havana. You are in New Orleans! We are a very special city full of unique things."

"Bernard, I think you are the one who is confused. That sounds like Havana to me, friend."

"Ramito, look over there. This is New Orleans. People take rides in carriages around the French Quarter here."

"Buddy, here in Havana, people ride in carriages all the time!"

"¡Ramito!" gritó Bernard. "Estás confundido. No estás en la Habana Vieja. ¡Estás en Nueva Orleans! Somos una ciudad muy especial llena de cosas únicas."

"Bernard, creo que tu eres el que está confundido. Eso me suena a mi como la Habana, asere."

"Ramito, mira allá. Esta es Nueva Orleans. Aquí la gente toma paseos en carruajes por el barrio francés."

"¡Asere, aquí en la Habana, la gente siempre viaja en carruajes!"

"In New Orleans, we do things like nowhere else," said Bernard. "Do people in Havana eat beans and rice on Mondays?"

"Buddy, you must be kidding. Here in Havana, people eat beans and rice every day, not just Monday!"

"En Nueva Orleans, hacemos cosas como ningún otro lugar," dijo Bernard. "¿Comen la gente arroz con frijoles en la Habana los lunes?"

"Asere, debes estar bromeando. ¡Aquí en la Habana, la gente come arroz con frijoles todos los días, no solo los lunes!"

Bernard pointed down the street. "Ramito, the people of New Orleans love to celebrate. There is always a party going on here. Do you hear the jazz music? Do you see the people dancing in the street?"

Ramito laughed. "Oh, what a joker you are! In Havana, there is always a celebration, with dancing and jazz!"

Bernard señaló calle abajo. "Ramito, a la gente de Nueva Orleans le encanta celebrar. Siempre hay una fiesta aquí. ¿Escuchas la música de jazz? ¿Ves a la gente bailando en la calle?"

Ramito se rió. "¡Ay, que chistoso eres! ¡En la Habana, siempre hay una gozadera, con bailes y jazz!"

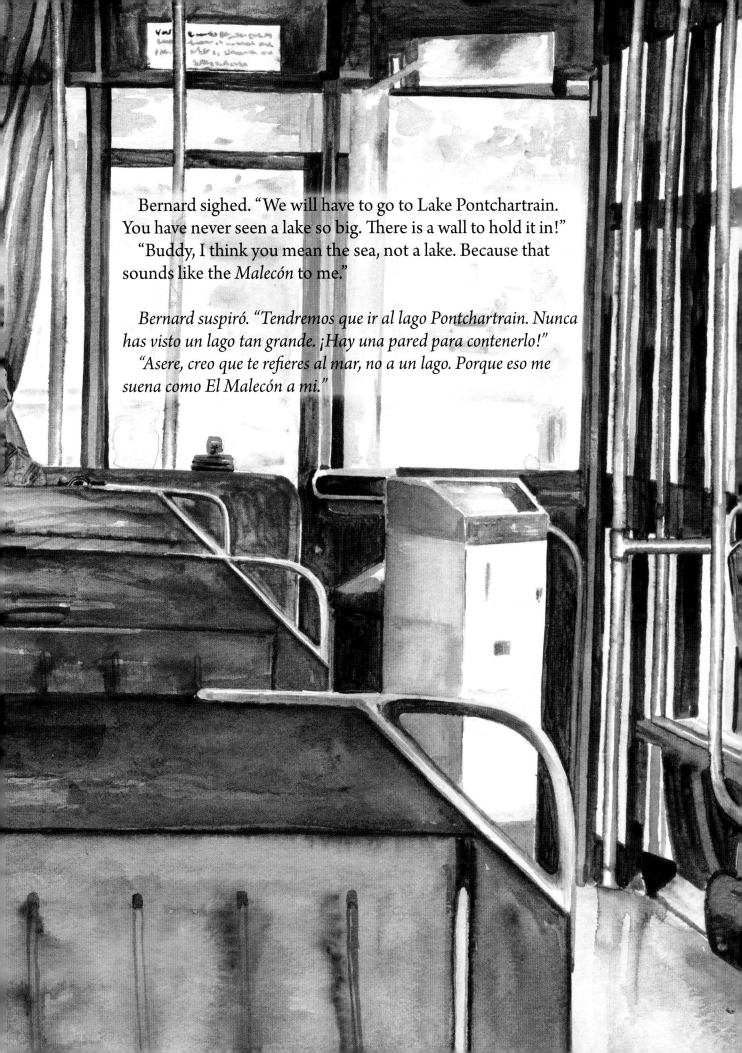

Bernard sighed. "We will have to go to Lake Pontchartrain. You have never seen a lake so big. There is a wall to hold it in!"

"Buddy, I think you mean the sea, not a lake. Because that sounds like the *Malecón* to me."

Bernard suspiró. "Tendremos que ir al lago Pontchartrain. Nunca has visto un lago tan grande. ¡Hay una pared para contenerlo!"

"Asere, creo que te refieres al mar, no a un lago. Porque eso me suena como El Malecón a mi."

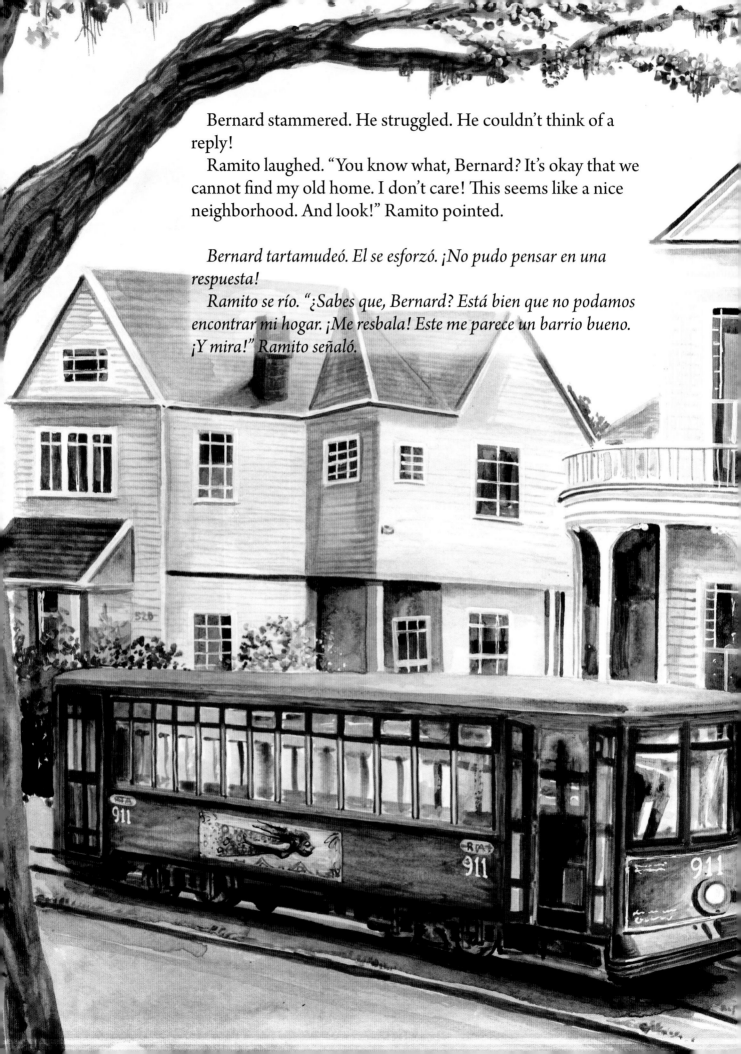

Bernard stammered. He struggled. He couldn't think of a reply!

Ramito laughed. "You know what, Bernard? It's okay that we cannot find my old home. I don't care! This seems like a nice neighborhood. And look!" Ramito pointed.

Bernard tartamudeó. El se esforzó. ¡No pudo pensar en una respuesta!

Ramito se río. "¿Sabes que, Bernard? Está bien que no podamos encontrar mi hogar. ¡Me resbala! Este me parece un barrio bueno. ¡Y mira!" Ramito señaló.

"There is a tree just as nice as my old Ceiba tree. I think I will stay in this new part of Havana. Thank you, my friend!"

"Hay un árbol igual de agradable que mi Ceiba vieja. Creo que me quedaré en esta parte nueva de la Habana. ¡Gracias, mi amigo!"

Bernard couldn't believe it! He could not think of one word to say. Was this really Havana? Were Havana and New Orleans the same *ciudad*? Why was he thinking *en español*?

¡Bernard no podía creerlo! No podía pensar en una palabra para decir. ¿Era esto realmente la Habana? ¿Era la Habana y Nueva Orleans la misma ciudad? ¿Por qué estaba pensando en español?

"Sorry, Ramito. I must go. Enjoy your new home."

"Lo siento, Ramito. Tengo que irme. Disfruta tu nueva casa."

Bernard yawned. "I just got very tired."

Bernard bostezó. "Estoy muy cansado."

"Tengo que surnar. I have to sleep."

AUTHOR'S NOTE

New Orleans and Havana have a rich shared history and culture. New Orleans is often called the "northernmost Caribbean city." From the vibrant jazz scenes and Spanish-colonial architecture to the food and weather, the two multicultural port cities have so much in common. The first modern Cuban flag to be raised there, in 1850, had been sewn and flown in New Orleans. Today, a statue of Cuban poet and revolutionary leader José Martí stands in the Mid-City neighborhood of New Orleans.

When illustrator Ramiro Díaz arrived in New Orleans, shortly after immigrating to the United States from his native Havana, he was amazed how much the city felt like home. He saw similarities everywhere. From that and an incident when the author's mother accidentally carried a hitchhiking lizard in her suitcase back to Pennsylvania after a visit to New Orleans, *¿Que Vola, NOLA? What's Up, NOLA?* was born.